Published by Boulder Publications
Portugal Cove-St. Philip's, Newfoundland and Labrador
www.boulderpublications.ca

© 2016 Joannie Smith Coffin and Brent Coffin

A portion of author royalties will be donated to the Bay St. George Sick Children's Foundation and the Janeway
Children's Hospital Foundation.

Design and layout: Sarah Hansen

Printed in Canada

Library and Archives Canada Cataloguing in Publication

Coffin, Joannie, 1955-, author
        The best Christmas ever / Joannie Coffin ; Brent Coffin, illustrator.

ISBN 978-1-927099-83-4 (hardback)

        I. Coffin, Brent, 1984-, illustrator II. Title.

PS8605.O3385B47 2016   jC813'.6   C2016-905569-8

We acknowledge the financial support of the Government of Newfoundland and Labrador through the Department of
Tourism, Culture and Recreation.

We acknowledge the financial support for our publishing program by the Government of Canada and the Department
of Canadian Heritage through the Canada Book Fund.

The Best CHRISTMAS Ever

Joannie Smith Coffin & Brent Coffin

On an island far
north in the Atlantic
Ocean lies the
snowy outport kingdom
of Hopewell. The proud
people of Hopewell live
off the sea, fishing from
schooners and small skiffs
to feed their families.

Rows of jellybean-
coloured houses lead to the
busy harbour. Bravestone
Head, a rugged mount
(and one of the four
corners of the world!),
watches over the kingdom.

Lighthouse Castle
perches at the top of
Bravestone Head. Its bright
light leads sailors home
through darkness and
storms.

In the Lighthouse Castle lived Princess Amari. She was kind and beloved by everyone in Hopewell. Her laughter could make the red pitcher plants bloom amid the winter snow. Her best friends were a lively group of animals who would do anything for the princess.

But the princess had been unwell. Even the best doctors from across the sea had not been able to find a cure for her illness. The flowers were wilting, and sadness had set in throughout the kingdom.

The princess had one wish: to hear the joyful sounds of laughter and singing among the people of Hopewell once again.

The king called an important meeting several weeks before Christmas. Princess Amari, bundled in thick blankets made by the Ladies Quilting Group and surrounded by her animal friends, sat upon a sturdy fish flake at the front of the gathering.

The king stepped forward. He declared the start of a contest, to make his daughter's wish come true. It would be called "The Best Christmas Ever."

A ripple of excitement went through the crowd. Everyone wanted to help the princess—and everyone loved a contest. Imaginations were set alight!

Santa and Mrs. Claus watched the king's announcement closely. They were always sad when children were ill. They decided to make an early visit to Hopewell to see if they could lend a hand.

First, they went to see what the Society of Knighted Fishers was working on. The Society's entry was a Tropical Christmas ... but it was a disaster.

Santa was not happy with his new flowery shirt. "Don't worry," said Mrs. Claus, "that overgrown beard of yours will hide it!" She was always after Santa to trim his unruly beard.

The palm trees imported for the contest bivvered in the snow and the reindeer didn't quite fit into their bathing suits. Dancer insisted that she have a designer hat flown in for the occasion— she had become a total diva since learning the latest funky square dance moves!

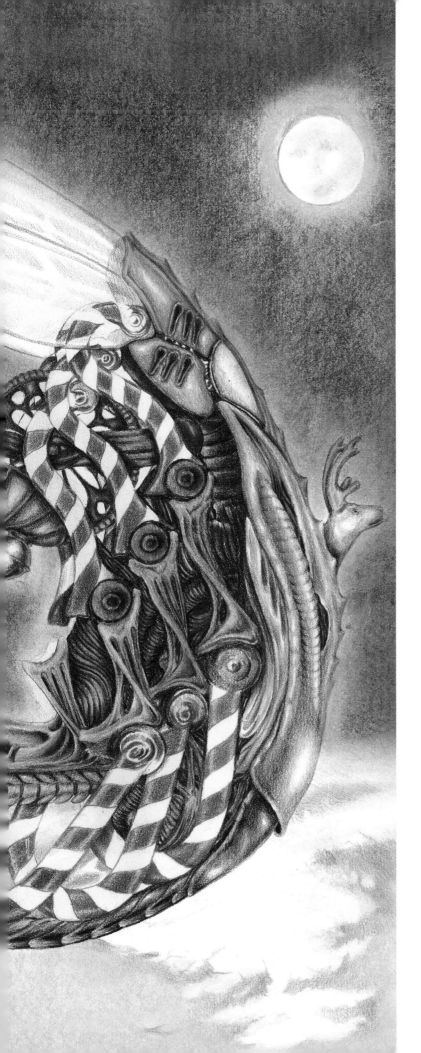

The next day, the Royal Marconi Council of Scientists of Hopewell declared a Christmas in space.

Mrs. Claus tried to help, welding plates of metal onto Santa's red space suit. It was too snug, and Santa's beard was chinched tightly into the helmet.

"Ack!" said Mrs. Claus, "your snarbuckle of a beard is hiding your rosy cheeks!"

To go with Santa's new space suit, the scientists created a sonic space sleigh with rocket boosters to launch it into orbit.

Outraged, the Reindeer Union staged a protest. They said the rocket boosters would take away their job pulling Santa's sleigh. Some of the reindeer chained themselves to the rocket boosters and held up protest signs.

The scientists hadn't meant to make the reindeer angry. They just wanted to build a cool space sleigh. They scrapped the rocket boosters and shook the reindeer's hooves—no hard feelings.

The members of the Royal Skiff Society wanted a deep-sea Christmas. They spent mountains of money to make a submarine sleigh.

The reindeer tried their best to pull the sleigh using propeller backpacks. Santa sat in a glass bubble that filled up with his ever-growing beard.

Octavia the octopus saw Santa's beard and thought it was another octopus. She wrapped all eight arms around the bubble and Santa. The giant hug took Santa's breath away.

"Back to the surface!" gasped Santa. "And get me some shears to cut this beard!"

Princess Amari's animal friends decided to create their own contest entry. Brandi and Brutus, the regal pit bulls, knew that the princess didn't care for expensive gimmicks.

"Clunky spaceships and rusty submarine sleighs aren't going to win," agreed Dobber-Bob the toy pug.

"And they've ruined Santa's wardrobe," moaned Abby the speckled boxer puppy.

"Who can save Christmas?" asked Levi the lop-eared bunny.

"We have to!" squawked Eedie the know-it-all emu.

"Well, let's waddle!" quacked Baby Duck.

Off they went in search of something to help them with their plan. First, they went to old Pad's shed at the end of Puffin Point. Nothing there—just Molly the horse, who was napping with one eye open. Next, they visited the boarded-up one-room schoolhouse. As the animals pried open the door, they glimpsed the old pot-bellied stove before the dust and ashes on the floor sent them into fits of coughing and sneezing.

Finally, the animals went to the tumble-down store by the community cellar. They peeked through the front door and saw a gigantic form covered with a sheet made of flour sacks.

Yelp! Squawk! Quack! What was it!?

"Ahhh! It's the Abominable-ble-ble Snowman!" squealed Abby.

With a loud *wooop!*, Eedie flew right at the monster to protect her friends. She hauled off the sheet, revealing a huge wooden sled that had not been used in years.

This gave the animals an amazing idea!

... But first, they had to rescue Eedie from the sheet that she was tangled in.

On Christmas Eve, the people of Hopewell gathered by the harbour for the Best Christmas Ever contest. Who could win?

Suddenly, a booming "HO HO HO MERRRRY CHRISTMAS!" was heard. The crowd parted to reveal the old wooden sled decked in Christmas ivy and holly. Santa was at the helm and the lively animals were playing among the heap of presents.

Princess Amari couldn't believe her eyes! Santa and all her friends had done this for her? She smiled brighter and wider than she had for months.

She was carried through the crowd by Sir John, a fisher knighted for his loyalty.

The king lifted the princess atop the old wooden sled, just as he had when she was younger.

Princess Amari suddenly remembered a game that she'd played as a child.

She used to sit on that old wooden sled and pretend that she had the power to bring great joy to the whole world. Her animal friends remembered the game too.

The princess thanked her friends for their gift and for bringing to mind such treasured memories.

As Santa placed Princess Amari's hands on the reins of the old wooden sled, she joyfully declared that this truly was the best Christmas ever!

The old wooden sled took flight. It whisked through the hills and marshes and the princess's laughter was heard by everyone in Hopewell.

The people were overcome with happiness and forgot their differences. They sang and danced around the Lighthouse Castle till the wee hours of the morning.

As the princess grew tired, Molly brought the old wooden sled around to the Castle Lighthouse entrance. Princess Amari smiled, blew a kiss, and waved before heading inside.

As winter passed, spring flowers began to bloom. The princess grew stronger, and her cheeks became a little rosier.

She was grateful every time she heard the sounds of laughter from her people. She loved being out in the gardens, sometimes getting out of her wheelchair to sit on a bench with Eedie the emu.

The princess decided to think only about the good things. It made her feel better. She smiled when Eedie fussed over her in the garden and when Brandi and Brutus rolled their eyes at Eedie. She had so much to be happy about.

While Nurse Maggie and the doctors kept a close eye on the princess, changes were taking place throughout Hopewell. Women and men were once again busily spreading fish on the flakes to dry for the winter. Others chatted over the clotheslines as they hung out Monday's wash.

Sounds of whistling and singing could be heard up and down the lanes as the older children carried yaffles of splits and buckets of water to their homes. Little ones were playing games of hide and seek and piddly. The flowers bloomed brighter than ever before.

And so it was, the magical old wooden sled won the Best Christmas Ever contest.

It sent the message to all that working together and helping others truly does create joy and hope.

May every Christmas be the best Christmas ever!

DEDICATIONS

Joannie: This book is dedicated to a princess who embodied the true meaning of grace and selflessness in the face of adversity and to a boy who made an "old lady's" dream come true.

Brent: To Matthew, my loving husband, who always supports and inspires my creativity. And to my girly dog, Abby, who has found her way to the centre of many images in this book.

JOANNIE SMITH COFFIN lives in Stephenville, Newfoundland and Labrador, with her husband, Garry. A retired health care professional, she is now an active volunteer in her community and an advocate for social justice issues. An avid reader and occasional writer for professional and social newsletters, Joannie discovered many years ago the value of sharing a message through storytelling. It is Joannie's wish that Princess Amari's story will show others how hope, goodwill, and imagination can bring moments of joy, even under the most difficult circumstances.

BRENT COFFIN studied Fine Art at Sir Wilfred Grenfell College in Corner Brook and the University College of Falmouth in England. Having focused on oil painting and fabric art for the last decade, it was refreshing for him to return to drawing with coloured leads for this book. Co-writing this story with his mother and illustrating it has opened up a whole new path for Brent and his work: the fusing of words and images to create a magical world. Brent lives in Mount Pearl, Newfoundland and Labrador, with his husband, Matthew, and dog, Abby.